NODDY AND THE WOODEN HORSE

NOW once when Noddy was driving along a country road his car suddenly made a peculiar noise, and then stopped.

"Good gracious! What's wrong with you?" said Noddy, in alarm, and he got out to see. "Your wheels haven't got a puncture, you've plenty of petrol. Then WHY don't you go?"

"Parp-parp," said the car, dolefully, and gave a little rattle.

"I'll have to take you to the garage and get you mended," said Noddy. "Something has gone wrong. But dear me, I'll have to push you all the way because this is a very lonely place and there's nobody to help me."

So he began to push and push, and how he panted and puffed. "I should like an engine going up a hill!" said Noddy. "Oh dear, I shall never get you to the garage!"

He pushed the car round a corner of the lane, and then he suddenly heard a noise. "Hrrrrumph! Help! Hrrrrumph!"

"Now what can *that* be?" said Noddy, and he stood and listened.

"Nay-hay-hay-hay-hay! Hrrrrrumph! Help!"

"Why—it's a horse in trouble!" said Noddy, and he squeezed through the hedge to find it. Sure enough, in the field beyond was a small horse, neighing and snorting loudly.

"What's the matter?" called Noddy.

"I walked into this muddy bit," said the horse, "and look —my front legs have sunk down into the mud and I can't get them out!"

Noddy ran to him. "I'll pull you out!" he said. "What part of you shall I pull?"

"My tail," said the horse. "It's a very strong tail. Hold hard—pull. PULL! Pull HARDER. I'm coming. I'm coming!"

Noddy pulled hard at the wooden horse's tail, and, quite suddenly, the horse's front legs came out of the mud, and the horse sat down hard on Noddy.

"Oooh, don't!" said Noddy. "I'm squashed to nothing. Get up, wooden horse. Don't sit on me like this."

"Sorry," said the horse, and got up. "You are really very kind. It was lucky for me that you came by just then in your car."

"Yes, it was," said Noddy. "But I wasn't *in* my car. Something's gone wrong with it, and I've got to push it all the way into Toyland Village. Goodness, I shall be tired!"

"You needn't be," said the wooden horse. "I am quite used to pulling carts. I could pull your car for you, if you like, all the way to the garage! I'd be glad to do you a good turn, little Noddy."

"Oh *thank* you!" said Noddy. "How lucky I am! Come along—I'll get my ropes and tie you to the car. What fun!"

And now, there goes Noddy sitting in his car, steering it carefully, and the little wooden horse is walking in front, pulling it well. How everyone stares!

"Aren't I lucky?" calls little Noddy. "My car broke down—and I found a little wooden horse to pull it!"

"You *are* lucky, Noddy—but, you see, you're kind too, and kind people are *always* lucky!"

TOM KITTEN'S TRICK

ONE day Noddy thought he would go fishing and catch a big fish for his dinner.

"Then I will ask Big-Ears and Tessie Bear to dinner with me, and I shall feel very proud!" said Noddy. "I will go and ask Big-Ears now."

So he went knocking at Big-Ears' toadstool house. "Big-Ears—please come to dinner with me today. I am going to catch a big fish."

He asked little Tessie Bear too, and she was very pleased. "I'll come," she said. "And I'll help cook the dinner."

Well, Noddy set off with his rod and line, and soon he came to a big round pond. "I shall catch my fish here," he said, and he sat down on the bank and began to fish.

Soon along came little Tom Kitten and he grinned at Noddy. "There's no fish in that pond!" he said.

"You don't know anything about it!" said Noddy. "Go

away. You're always teasing people."

"Big-Ears is looking for you," said Tom Kitten. "He's over there."

Noddy put down his rod and ran to find Big-Ears at once. Naughty Tom grinned. He knew that Big-Ears wasn't anywhere near—he just wanted to play a little trick on Noddy!

Do you know what he did? He had seen an old boot in the pond, and he quickly waded in and what did he do but fix that boot to the end of Noddy's line! How he laughed!

Noddy came back, very cross! "Big-Ears wasn't looking

for me. He wasn't anywhere to be seen, you bad kitten.''

He picked up his rod—and dear me, he felt something on the end of the line at once! ''A fish! I've got a fish!'' he cried. ''My goodness me, it's a BIG one!''

Noddy pulled and pulled, trying to bring up the big fish—and at last up it came. There was the boot, dangling on the end of his line.

Tom Kitten rolled over and over on the grass and laughed till he cried. ''Ho, ho, ho! *I* put it there! You thought it was a great big fish! Oh, what a tale. I'll tell everyone in the village!''

''You're very unkind,'' said Noddy. ''I thought it was such a big fish—and I was going to cook it for dinner and I've asked Big-Ears and Tessie Bear. . . ."

"Ho, ho, ho!" laughed Tom Kitten. "I'll go and tell them they'll have fried boot for dinner, with boot-lace sauce!"

"Hallo—what's all this noise about?" suddenly said a voice, and up came big Mr. Burly Bear. "Why, little Noddy —I *do* believe you've caught the boot I lost in the pond last

winter when I skated on it and the ice broke! I fell in and lost one of my boots —and here it is back again! I shall dry it out and wear it again. Noddy, you really are very, very clever!"

"Am I?" said Noddy, and his head nodded up and down fast because he was very pleased.

"You are," said Mr. Burly Bear. "Look, here is a whole pound for catching my boot. You go and buy a fish at the fishmonger's and give a little party."

"Oh, *thank* you!" cried Noddy "I'll go this very minute. Ha, ha, Tom Kitten—you played a trick on me, but *you're* the one that looks silly now!''

And off he went to buy a nice big fish for dinner. Look— he's in his little house, cooking it now, with little Tessie Bear to help him, and Big-Ears is laying the table.

''We're going to have a very nice time,'' said Noddy. ''And all because I caught a boot instead of a great big fish!''

A BAG OF MIXED SPELLS

One day Miss Fluffy Cat came to ask Noddy to take her to Magic Village in his little car. They set out, and Miss Fluffy Cat told Noddy that she badly wanted to get herself a new tail there.

Noddy had never been to Magic Village, so he felt quite excited. "Here we are," said Miss Fluffy Cat.

Magic Village was full of little crooked cottages and queer towers and strange little shops.

While Miss Fluffy Cat went to get herself a new tail, Noddy looking in at the shop windows. What queer things he saw!

"I'll buy something to take home!" he thought. "I'll buy a bag of Mixed Spells, and try them. What fun!"

A BAG OF MIXED SPELLS

He bought the bag of Mixed Spells, and then Miss Fluffy Cat called him. "I'm ready to go home," she said. She had had a most beautiful new tail put on by magic, and she wore her old tail for a fur. She really looked nice.

They set off home and Noddy told Miss Fluffy Cat about his Mixed Spells. "You be careful!" she said.

They got back to Toyland Village and Miss Fluffy Cat paid him six pence. Her new tail waved about proudly.

"I think I'll go to tea with Big-Ears and take this bag of Mixed Spells to show him," said Noddy.

Big-Ears was very pleased to see him. "Come in," he said. "What have you got there, little Noddy?"

A BAG OF MIXED SPELLS

"A bag of Mixed Spells!" said Noddy, and shook a lot of little coloured boxes on to the table.

Big-Ears picked one up. "Vanishing pill," he read on the lid. He took out a small yellow pill.

But it slipped from his fingers to the floor—and in a trice Big-Ears' big black cat had pounced on it . . .

And swallowed it. BANG! She disappeared at once, and only a little bit of white smoke showed where she'd been!

"Oh! My cat! She's gone!" cried Big-Ears. "Your silly spells, Noddy—now see what's happened!"

"Well, *you* dropped it!" said Noddy. He went down on his hands and knees, calling, "Puss, Puss, Puss!"

A BAG OF MIXED SPELLS

But no cat came, of course. Noddy stood up and took another box from the table. "Perhaps," he began . . .

But Big-Ears was so upset and angry that he threw the rest of the boxes into the fire!

BANG! POP! BANG! Fizzle-whoosh, fizzle! BANG! Whatever was happening! Noddy ran outside in fright.

And will you believe it, as he stood there, Big-Ears' toadstool house began to melt . . ."

Yes, it melted just as if it had been made of snow. Noddy called to Big-Ears. "Where are you?"

But nobody answered. The toadstool house melted all away, and left nothing but a queer, slushy puddle . . .

A BAG OF MIXED SPELLS

That ran round Noddy's feet, and felt as sticky as treacle. Oh dear, oh dear, what a dreadful thing!

Poor Noddy jumped into his car, crying big tears, and drove off to Miss Fluffy Cat's. She might help him.

"How silly you are to play about with spells!" she said. "Are there any left, little Noddy?"

"No," said Noddy, and then he remembered the one he had picked up from the table. "Yes, this one," he said.

"Ah—this is a Come-Back Spell," said Miss Fluffy Cat. "Go back and throw it on Big-Ears' melted house."

So back went Noddy at top speed. Here he is at the spot where the toadstool house melted before his eyes!

He threw the Come-Back Spell into the treacly mess—and hey presto, see what is happening!

There is the big toadstool stalk growing—and now the top comes—and now the little chimney . . .

And then the window—and the door! Noddy ran to it and opened it—was dear old Big-Ears inside?

Yes, he was, looking most surprised. "Whatever happened?" he said. "Oh, there's my old cat back again!"

"Oh what a good thing I had that one spell left!" said Noddy, hugging Big-Ears. "What a very good thing!"

"I'll never buy spells again, Big-Ears. Oh, I'm glad you're back!" And now do look at him dancing with the cat!

GILBERT GOLLY IS VERY NAUGHTY

NODDY was cleaning his car one day when Gilbert Golly came along. He didn't go too near because he knew that Noddy didn't like him very much and might turn the hose on him.

"Noddy," he said, staring up at Noddy's roof, "it seems to me as if one of your chimneys is loose."

"It isn't," said Noddy.

"You ought just to have a look at it and make sure," said Gilbert Golly. "It might fall off and hit someone."

"I haven't a ladder," said Noddy. "And I can't borrow Mr. Tubby Bear's next door because he's out. He doesn't like me to take things without asking."

"I can get one for you," said Gilbert Golly.

"You're very kind all of a sudden!" said little Noddy, his head nodding up and down. "What's come over you?"

"Oh—I just *feel* kind, that's all," said Gilbert. "It won't be any trouble to get you a ladder, Noddy. I can borrow one from my Uncle Whiskers. He lives just up the road."

"All right," said Noddy, looking up at his chimney, which seemed quite all right to him. Still, it would never do to risk it falling down on dear old Big-Ears or Mrs. Tubby Bear.

Gilbert Golly went off up the road. He knew that his Uncle Whiskers was up on his roof mending a loose tile and had got his ladder. Yes, there it was, leaning against the wall.

Gilbert didn't like his Uncle Whiskers and his uncle didn't like Gilbert. He was always willing to give Gilbert a good spanking and Gilbert kept out of his way, waiting and waiting for a chance to tease his uncle.

He looked up at the roof. Yes—his uncle was sitting up there with his back to him, very busy with the loose tile. Gilbert ran for the ladder!

He slid it away from the wall and ran off with it down the road to little Noddy's house, hearing the bang-bang-bang, tap-tap-tap of his uncle's mallet on the roof. Uncle Whiskers didn't see Gilbert at all.

Gilbert gave Noddy the ladder. "My Uncle Whiskers was

NODDY EXAMINES THE CHIMNEYS ON HIS ROOF

very pleased to lend it to you,'' he said. ''And he says you can keep it till to-morrow if you like.''

''That's very kind of him,'' he said, sur-prised. ''I'll go up and look at my chimney now. Thanks, Gilbert Golly. Go and cut yourself some of the chocolate cake in my larder.''

Gilbert cut himself an enormous slice and ran out again, giggling to himself. He went back up the road to his Uncle Whiskers' house, munching the cake. He stood there watching his uncle up on the roof.

Soon his uncle finished his job and looked for the ladder. It wasn't there! He gave a yell. ''Where's my ladder? What's happened to my ladder?''

''Tisn't here, Uncle!'' called Gilbert Golly. ''Are you

sure you didn't take it up on the roof with you?''

''Don't be silly!'' shouted his uncle. ''WHERE is it? Look all round the house, Gilbert.''

Gilbert went all round and came back. ''No, it's not there,'' he said. ''But I know where it is. I saw it at little Noddy's house.''

His uncle almost fell off the roof in surprise.

''At little *Noddy's* house! What's it doing there?''

''I don't know. I think Noddy's looking to see if his chimney's loose,'' said Gilbert, munching away at his cake. ''I expect he borrowed it, Uncle.''

''Borrowed it!'' roared Uncle Whiskers, in a rage. ''Borrowed it while I was sitting up here on the roof! What's come over little Noddy? Just wait till I get him! I'll give him such a good spanking, I'll . . .''

''But how are you going to get him, Uncle?'' said Gilbert Golly. ''It looks to me as if you'll be sitting up there on your roof all night long.''

''You go straight to little Noddy's house and tell him to bring back my ladder!'' shouted Uncle Whiskers. ''At once!''

''Noddy wouldn't do anything *I* told him,'' said Gilbert. ''Anyway, I'm tired. I don't want to go all the way to his house.''

"Gilbert!" said his uncle, in a very, very fierce voice. "Gilbert, if I were not sitting up here on the roof, do you know what I would do to you?"

"Well, I could guess!" said Gilbert. "But you'd much better throw me down six pence for some sweets, Uncle. Then I might go and tell Noddy to bring the ladder back then."

There was nothing for it but to throw Gilbert Golly six pence. It trickled down the roof and fell to the ground. Gilbert picked it up.

"Thank you, Uncle. I'll just go and buy the sweets then if I'm not too tired I'll go and tell little Noddy about the ladder," he said, and off went the bad golly to the sweet-shop.

He grinned to himself. He had told Noddy not to take the ladder back till the next day and it was nice to think of his uncle sitting up on the roof all night. Nobody lived near him, so they wouldn't hear his shouts.

"And certainly *I'm* not going to tell Noddy to take back the ladder!" he thought. "My goodness me, how clever I am! What a joke this is!"

But Gilbert Golly forgot that Big-Ears had taught Noddy to return borrowed things at once. So, when he had seen his chimney wasn't loose, he struggled up the road to return the ladder to Gilbert's uncle.

What a roar greeted him! "HO! So you've brought my ladder back, have you? How DARE you borrow it when I'm up on my roof? Here I've been sitting and . . ."

"Gilbert said

you'd finished with it and would be glad to lend it to me!" said Noddy, surprised. "I'm sorry, very very, sorry, very, very, very..." "That will do," said Uncle Whiskers. "Just you wait until I get down, then I'll show you what it feels like to be sorry."

"Mr. Whiskers, please believe me," said Noddy. "I did NOT come and take your ladder. It was a trick of Gilbert's."

Uncle Whiskers was so angry that he slid halfway down the roof in a rage, and only just managed to save himself from falling. Noddy put the ladder up to him in alarm.

"Be careful! You nearly fell then! Oh, Mr. Whiskers, please don't be cross with me. I'm so very, very . . ."

But Mr. Whiskers had slid down the ladder at top speed and took no notice of Noddy at all. He raced off down the road in

the direction of the sweet-shop. Noddy stared after him in surprise.

"*Now* where's he going?" he said. "Really, Mr. Whiskers is a very peculiar person!"

I know where he's gone, don't you? What a dreadful shock Gilbert Golly will get when he sees his uncle coming into the sweet-shop. He will certainly wish he had never meddled with the ladder that afternoon!

See how well
you can paint
or crayon this
picture of Noddy
and Big-Ears
gardening

NODDY CLIMBS A TREE

"Here I go
In my little car,
Bumpity-bump,
How happy we are!"

THAT was the song little Noddy was singing as he drove through the woods. He had just taken Mrs. Golly to stay with her sister in Golly Town and now he was coming back at top speed through the trees.

The path was very rough—bumpity-bump went the car and Noddy bounced up and down in the driving seat.

"I feel as if I were riding on a horse!" he said. And then, quite suddenly, the little car stopped.

Noddy was surprised. "What's the matter with you?" he said. "I didn't make you stop. Have you got a puncture in one of your tyres?"

"Parp-parp-parp-parp-PARP!" said the little car, as if it wanted to tell Noddy something important. Noddy wondered what it could be saying. He looked all round him—and then he suddenly heard somebody shouting.

"Oh help, help! Oh, I shall fall! Oh, help, help!"

"Dear me—somebody's in trouble," said Noddy, and he got out of his car at once. He stood and listened. Where was the shouting coming from?

"It seems to come from high up," said Noddy to himself. "Perhaps it's somebody up in a tree?"

So he went to look up the trees—and then, high up in a big tree he saw something blue. He looked and he looked, and then he saw little Connie Kitten in her blue dress.

"Connie Kitten! What's happened?" he called.

"Oh, is that you, little Noddy?" shouted Connie Kitten. "Please help me! I've climbed up this tree and I daren't get down. I just daren't!"

"Good gracious! Whatever did you climb it for then?" asked Noddy, climbing up himself.

"Well, a bird called something rude after me and I thought I would climb up to its nest and take its eggs," said Connie.

"That wasn't very nice of you," said Noddy. "You shouldn't take birds' eggs, you know that."

"Well, I wish I hadn't climbed up now," said Connie Kitten, beginning to cry. "I'm frightened. I couldn't reach the nest, and now that horrid bird is laughing at me."

"Well, look—put your foot just *here*," said little Noddy, taking hold of Connie Kitten's ankle and pulling it gently down to a lower branch.

But she screamed loudly and clutched the trunk of the tree tightly. "No, no—I shall fall, I know I shall. You must carry me down."

"Don't be silly, I can't do that," said Noddy. "I'm not big enough. Look—just tread *here*, and then . . ."

"No!" squealed Connie Kitten. "I'm afraid of climbing down. Get somebody to come and carry me down."

"All right," said Noddy and began to climb down. "I must say that I think you are very silly, Connie Kitten."

When he was halfway down Connie squealed again. "I'm falling! I feel giddy! I shall fall right down and hurt myself. Come back, Noddy, and hold me."

Noddy climbed back as fast as he could. Connie Kitten had her eyes closed and she certainly looked frightened! Noddy put his arm round her.

"Don't fall. Don't let go. I'm holding you. But how can I get help if I have to stay up here with you and hold you all the time, Connie Kitten?" he said.

"I don't know," said Connie, clutching at Noddy and almost making him lose his balance. "I know I shall fall! Oh, why did I think I could climb a tree—and in my new dress, too!"

Noddy suddenly had a very good idea. He took his scarf and put it round a nearby branch—and he put it round Connie Kitten too! He knotted his nice yellow scarf tightly—and there was Connie Kitten, tied fast to a branch!

"There!" said little Noddy, pleased. "You're quite safe

now, Connie. Even if you fall, the scarf will hold you up. Don't be afraid any more. I'm going to climb down and get Big-Ears, my friend, to come and rescue you. He's very strong."

"I do think you're clever, little Noddy!" said Connie.

Noddy climbed down the tree again and ran to his car. "I'll soon come back with Big-Ears!" he said, and away he went to Big-Ears' toadstool house.

Big-Ears was at home, which was lucky. "Come at once, Big-Ears!" cried Noddy. "Connie Kitten's up a tree and she can't get down! I've tied her tightly to a branch with my scarf, but she feels very, very giddy."

"Dear me—that Connie Kitten is always getting into some fix or other!" said Big-Ears, and he got into Noddy's car. Off they went.

Noddy drove to the big tree and called loudly. "Connie Kitten! Here we are. Big-Ears is going to climb up and carry you down."

There was no answer, so Noddy called again and Big-Ears got out of the car. He peered up the tree.

"No wonder there isn't an answer!" he said. "There's nobody there. It must be the wrong tree!"

"It isn't, it isn't!" said Noddy, and he got out to look too. But dear me, no Connie Kitten was there!

"Drive your car round and about and shout," said Big-Ears, rather cross. So Noddy drove round and yelled at the top of his voice. But no Connie Kitten answered.

NODDY DROVE HIS CAR ROUND AND ABOUT AND SHOUTED

"It was just a joke she played on you!" said Big-Ears. "She must have climbed down as soon as you had gone, and run home laughing—with your nice yellow scarf!"

"Goodness me—the horrid kitten!" said Noddy in a rage. "I'm going to Connie Kitten's home right now and give her a good smacking!"

And dear me, off he went in a dreadful temper. Look out, Connie Kitten—here comes a very angry Noddy!

He came to Connie Kitten's house and banged the door—blam, blam, blam! He put a big frown on his face, and his head nodded very fast indeed—nid-niddy-nod-nid-niddy-nod!

The door opened—and there was Connie Kitten, all smiles! "Oh, it's *you*, Noddy! I was just ironing your scarf, ready to bring it back to you, it was so crumpled with knots. My uncle, Mr. Whiskers Cat, came by just after you had gone, and untied me and lifted me down."

"Oh," said Noddy, and his frown flew off his face at once.

"I thought perhaps you had been playing a horrid trick on me, Connie Kitten."

"Oh *no*! I just wanted to iron your scarf—and look, I bought you a nice little scarf-pin on my way back," said Connie, showing him a beautiful scarf-pin. "I was going to call at your house and leave them for you. Oh, Noddy, I *do* think you are clever—nobody else but you would ever have thought of tying me to the tree with a scarf!"

Noddy was very, very pleased. "I was going to be cross and smack you," he said, "but now I am pleased and I want to buy you an ice-cream. Get into my car and we'll go."

"Put your scarf on first," said Connie, and he put it on and proudly put in his new scarf-pin. Off they go—and I can hear him singing his little song!

"Here we go in my little car,
    Bumpity-bump, how happy we are!"

NODDY, BIG-EARS AND MR. WOBBLY MAN HAVE BEEN PICKING APPLES. CAN YOU GUESS WHO HAS PICKED MOST?

"HEY, Noddy, hey! Take me to the market!" shouted a teddy bear who was standing at the corner of the street with a sack as Noddy came by in his little car.

Noddy stopped. "Hallo, Mr. Bear," he said. "Get in. Put your sack at the back."

"What do you charge to go to the market?" asked the bear. Noddy didn't like him very much. He was rather dirty and his coat was torn.

"Six pence," said Noddy, setting off. They hadn't gone very far before Noddy heard a little noise behind—bump-bumpity, bump.

"What's that?" he said.

"Oh, nothing," said the bear. "The road is so bumpy that the car makes quite a noise."

"All the same I'm sure I can hear something going bumpity-bump," said Noddy. "As if something was falling down from the car. I do hope it's not falling to bits."

"Of course not," said the bear. "Please don't stop, Noddy—I really must get to market quickly. I've some *beautiful* big apples in my sack, freshly picked this morning and I'm going to sell them for a lot of money."

Now the bear was telling a naughty story. He *hadn't* got apples in his bag! He only had potatoes, and not very good ones either! He also had something else in that sack—a big hole! He had cut one there himself, so that the potatoes would fall out one by one as Noddy took him along in his little car. What a peculiar thing to do!

They came to the market and then Mr. Bear got out and went to collect his sack. He gave a loud yell.

"What's the matter?" said N o d d y, anxiously.

"My apples! My BEAUTI-

FUL apples! There's not a single one left in the sack!'' cried Mr. Bear. ''Not one. They must have fallen out every time you went over a bump, Noddy. That's the worst of a silly car like this—it has such bad springs that not even apples in a sack are safe!''

''My car is a very good one!'' said Noddy, fiercely. ''I *heard* something falling into the road, but you wouldn't let me stop. I'm sorry about it, but it's NOT my fault!''

''It *is*,'' said Mr. Bear, looking very fierce too. ''Because of your silly bumpy car I've lost all my apples—and I should have sold them for twenty pounds.''

''You would not,'' said Noddy.

''I would,'' said Mr. Bear. ''But as I don't expect you've got much money, I will only charge you ten pounds for losing them out of your car.''

''Ten pounds! I've only got *two* pounds!'' said Noddy. ''And I'm not going to give you that. *You* owe me six pence for taking you to the market!''

"We'll tell Mr. Plod," said Mr. Bear, and he beckoned to the policeman, who was standing in the market, directing traffic.

Mr. Plod listened to Mr. Bear's tale. "ALL my beautiful apples gone!" he wailed. "And all because of his bumpy car. I'm very kind only to charge him ten pounds."

"You must pay up, Noddy," said Mr. Plod. "Pay the two pounds you have and . . ."

Just then Big-Ears rode up panting on his bicycle. He had a very big basket in front, because it was his shopping day. It was full to the brim with old potatoes.

"Hey, Noddy!" he called. "I've been trying to catch you up for ages. I was riding be-hind your car and I saw these potatoes falling out of a sack at the back. So I picked them up, put them in my basket —and here they are. You

must have a big hole in that sack!"

"*Potatoes!*" cried Noddy. "But Mr. Bear said they were his very best apples. Oooh, you fibber, Mr. Bear!"

Mr. Plod suddenly caught hold of Mr. Bear.

"Ha!" he said. "This needs looking into! You've been tricking our little Noddy—you put old potatoes into a sack with a hole in it and said they were good apples. You're a bad bear. Now you just pay Noddy a whole pound for his trouble, put your old potatoes into your sack and carry them away to the rubbish-heap!"

Mr. Bear looked scared. He gave Noddy a pound, and Big-Ears emptied the potatoes into the sack. Mr. Bear put it on his back without a word and walked off with it.

Bumpity-bump! Bump-bump-bump!

Noddy gave a squeal of laughter. "Oh! He won't get far before his sack feels as light as can be! There go all his potatoes out of the hole, one by one!"

Bumpity-bump! It serves you right, Mr. Bear. You shouldn't play horrid tricks on people.

"Big-Ears, thank you very much!" said little Noddy. "I've got a pound instead of six pence! Let's go and spend it on ice-creams!"

So off they go together. Good old Big-Ears—he really is a help to little Noddy, isn't he?

BAD MISTER GRAB

One day, when Noddy was just finishing his breakfast, a knock came at his door. "Who is it?" called Noddy. "Someone come to hire your car," said a voice. "For a long journey!" Noddy went to the door at once.

Outside stood a queer-looking fellow, rather like one of the goblins who lived in the woods.

"I'm Mr. Grab," he said. "I want to go to Faraway Town." Noddy went to get his car.

"That's a very, very long way," he said. "Have you enough money to pay for such a long journey?"

Mr. Grab grinned. He opened a bag he carried and let Noddy look inside. It was full of shining gold money!

BAD MISTER GRAB

"My word—you *are* rich!" said Noddy. "Get in, please." Off they went, Mr. Grab sitting beside Noddy.

Now, when they came to a very lonely place, Mr. Grab ordered Noddy to stop the car. Noddy stopped it in surprise.

"Now get out," said Mr. Grab, "because *I* want your car," he said. "From now on it's *my* car!"

"It isn't!" cried Noddy, in alarm. "You're a bad goblin, Mr. Grab. I believe you stole that money. I *won't*——"

But dear me, the goblin gave poor Noddy a big push, and out he fell into the road. Then r-r-r-r-r-r . . .

Mr. Grab started the car again and raced away up the road at sixty miles an hour. Good gracious!

BAD MISTER GRAB

Noddy sat and wailed. "Oh dear! What am I to do? I don't know where I am, and my dear little car is stolen!"

Mr. Grab and the car were out of sight. Noddy walked along the road, shedding tears as if he were raining.

Another car came along the road. "Stop!" cried Noddy. The car stopped and a very smart toy dog looked out.

"Please will you chase a robber who has taken my car?" said Noddy. "Jump in," said Mr. Dog, and away they went.

But they couldn't see any sign of Mr. Grab. Mr. Dog set Noddy down even further from home than before!

"It's no good going after that goblin!" he thought sadly. "I'll have to walk all the way home!"

BAD MISTER GRAB

He got a lift on Master Bert Bear's motor-bicycle, but after Noddy's hat had blown off three times . . .

And Master Bear had to stop while he got it, Bert Bear turned him off, and went roaring away by himself.

Then Noddy got a lift in a farmer's hay-cart, but alas, he fell asleep and tumbled out of the cart . . .

And as the old farmer was deaf, he didn't hear him shouting—so there was Noddy all alone again!

He walked and he walked, and at last he came to a little railway station. But when the train came in . . .

It was going the wrong way, so Noddy set off walking again, thinking of all the things he would like to do to Mr. Grab!

BAD MISTER GRAB

And then what did he hear but a bicycle bell—and round the corner came dear old Big-Ears on his little bicycle!

He *was* surprised to see Noddy and hear his sad tale. "Get on my bicycle at the back and we'll fetch Mr. Plod," he said.

So here they go together, to find Mr. Plod. "Here's the police-station," says Noddy. "I'll knock!" blam-blam. Mr. Plod opened the door. "Oh Mr. Plod, my car has been stolen, and it must be in Faraway Town by now!" said Noddy.

"No, it isn't," said Mr. Plod, with a great big smile on his face. "Look!" And he opened a door, and . . .

There was Noddy's little car in Mr. Plod's sitting room! "I'll tell you how it came there," said Mr. Plod.

"It wouldn't take that bad Mr. Grab to Faraway Town. As soon as it came to a corner, it went the opposite way. And it came back here at top speed, so that Mr. Grab didn't dare to get out. It ran through my front door . . .

"And came hooting into my sitting room where I was sitting! I did get a shock! So I grabbed Mr. Grab . . .

"And now he's locked up in a cell, and I've got all the money he stole!" Noddy *was* surprised.

"You're the cleverest car in the world!" said Noddy, patting it. "Let's go home, Big-Ears, and have a fine tea."

And they drove right out of Mr. Plod's big front door, hooting loudly. Good gracious—HOW surprised everyone was!

THE CLOCKWORK MOUSE'S TAIL

ONCE a dear little clockwork mouse called Clicky came to live in Noddy's street. Noddy liked him very much. He ran up and down all day long, visiting here and visiting there, chattering to everyone in his little squeaky voice.

And then one day he came to Noddy looking very scared indeed. "Noddy," he said. "Please help me."

"What's the matter?" asked Noddy.

"Well, Dilly Duck is being very very unkind to me," said Clicky. "Every time she sees me, she waddles after me and tries to pick off my tail."

"Dilly Duck does that?" said Noddy, in surprise. "But she's a very kind toy duck. I can't believe it. If I see her doing such a thing I shall be very cross with her."

Well, the very next day, when Noddy was driving along in his car, he saw Clicky the mouse scampering down the street, squealing, and Dilly Duck after him, waddling at top speed.

Noddy stopped his car at once. He got out. "Dilly Duck!" he called, sternly. "How *dare* you chase the little clockwork mouse and peck his tail."

Dilly Duck stopped at once, and looked at little Noddy. "I'm not chasing Clicky," she said. "I'm chasing a worm —a nice long, wriggly worm!"

"But that's not a worm, that's Clicky's rubber tail!" said Noddy.

"Goodness me—is it really?" said Dilly Duck, peering down at it. "No —look, it's a worm, it's wriggling!" And she gave it a peck. Clicky squealed and ran to Noddy.

"There! She did it

again! One day she'll peck my tail right off and eat it. Smack her, Noddy. Take her to Mr. Plod the policeman. Lock her up. Horrid Dilly Duck!"

"Now, you must both come with me," said Noddy. "I'm going to buy you each something that will stop Dilly Duck from thinking your tail is a worm, and chasing it every time she sees you. Come along!"

Well, first he took them to a little shop kept by Mrs. Wooden Doll, who sold ribbons and pins and socks and buttons and things like that.

"I want a nice long piece of bright red ribbon," he said to Mrs. Wooden Doll, so she cut them some from a little red roll. Noddy took it and tied it round the clockwork mouse's tail, and made a fine big bow, right at the end of it.

"Doesn't my tail look grand?" said Clicky, pleased, and he twitched it so that the red bow jumped gaily about. "My tail thinks it must be going to a party!"

"Now, Dilly Duck, you'll not think Clicky's tail is a worm again," said Noddy, "because worms don't wear ribbons."

"Well—I *might*!" said Dilly Duck, peering at the lively tail. "I'm very short-sighted, you know."

"Yes, I know," said Noddy. "And that's why I'm going to buy *you* something too! Come along!"

He took Dilly Duck to the shop that sold eye-glasses, and he bought her a perfectly beautiful pair. She was *very* pleased.

"Don't I look GRAND!" she said, staring all round, with the glasses perched on her beak. "Oh, thank you, Noddy? I'll never think Clicky's tail is a worm again."

Clever little Noddy. No wonder his head nodded very fast indeed when he drove off again in his car!

NO WAG IN HIS TAIL

ONCE, when Noddy was out shopping, he met Mr. Waggy Dog. "Hallo!" said Noddy. "How are you, Waggy? I haven't seen you for a long time."

"Oh, things have gone very very wrong with me," said Waggy, sadly. "Didn't you hear? My chimney got on fire and burnt my roof off . . ."

"Gracious! What a thing to happen!" said Noddy.

"And then I got in a fight with Mr. Whiskers Cat," said Waggy, "and he bit both my ears off and I had to get Mrs. Wobbly to sew them on again."

"She's sewn them on crooked," said Noddy looking at them.

"And then I got a cold in my nose, and it felt like an elephant's trunk, it swelled up so," said Waggy.

"It still looks a bit funny," said Noddy.

"But worse than that, I've lost the wag out of my tail," said Waggy. "Look at it—not a wag in it! And what's the good of a tail without a wag?"

"Where did you lose the wag?" asked Noddy. "I'll go and look for it."

"I don't know," said Waggy dog. "It just disappeared, and now my tail won't wag any more. It hasn't the tiniest bit of a wag left. I feel very, very sad."

Noddy felt sad too. What dreadful things had happened to poor Waggy! He would try to find the wag for his tail.

Well, Noddy looked everywhere for the lost wag. He didn't quite know what it would look like, but he thought it would be hairy and would wag along the ground. The only thing he saw that might be a wag was a caterpillar, but it went down a hole. "Bother!" said Noddy. "I'll go and tell Big-Ears. Perhaps he's seen a lost wag somewhere."

So he got into his little car and drove off to Big-Ears' toad-stool house. He hooted outside, and big-Ears came to the door.

"Oh, I'm so pleased to see you," he said. "My black cat has gone to visit her Aunty Mew-Mew, and I do feel so lonely. Come in and have a ginger biscuit."

Noddy ate his ginger biscuit and told Big-Ears about Waggy Dog and all his bad luck. "And now he's lost the wag in his tail, and though I've looked for it everywhere, I can't find it," said Noddy. "I did think I saw it today, but it wriggled down a hole."

Big-Ears laughed. "All that Mr. Waggy Dog wants is a bit of good luck," he said. "You listen to me, now. Ask him to tea today. Pick some blackberries and put them in a basket to give him. Find that nice bit of red ribbon you never wear, and wash and iron it for Waggy's neck. Take some of these ginger biscuits and half my chocolate cake for tea. Buy a block of ice-cream, and . . ."

"Good gracious! All this sounds very nice," said Noddy, pleased. "But I still can't give him his lost wag, Big-Ears."

"You wait and see," said Big-Ears. "Now go and pick a basketful of blackberries, while I wrap up the chocolate cake and biscuits."

Well, that afternoon, Waggy dog came along to tea with Noddy, looking very sad. His tail hung behind him without a wag in it. He sat down solemnly and gazed at the tea-table.

"Ginger biscuits!" said Noddy.

"Oooh—chocolate cake!" said Waggy.

"Heaps of ice-cream," said Noddy.

"Ripe blackberries for me!" said Waggy.

"And see—a lovely bit of red ribbon for your furry neck," said Noddy.

Waggy beamed at him. Noddy tied the ribbon round his neck. "You look bee-yoo-tiful!" he said.

Waggy beamed again—then he suddenly lost his smile and got up off his chair. "I'm sitting on something funny," he said. "Was it your cat? It wriggled under me!"

MR. WAGGY DOG CAME TO TEA WITH NODDY

THE NEW BIG NODDY BOOK

BY
Enid Blyton

ISBN 0 361 06400 4
Copyright © 1984 Darrell Waters Limited as to the text herein
and Purnell Publishers Limited as to the artwork herein
Published 1984 by Purnell Books, Paulton, Bristol BS18 5LQ,
Member of the BPCC Group
Made and printed in Great Britain by Purnell and Sons
(Book Production) Limited, Paulton, Bristol,
Member of the BPCC Group